By Scott

Jake and Dixie

Super Magic Lightning Boy

THIS BOOK IS

Jake and Dixie are playing outside when Mum gives t_
new mission. They must go to the bottom of the garde_
find out what baddies are lurking there.

Super Magic Lightning Boy and Dixie Thunder Paws must be
brave and tough to fulfill their quest.

Illustrations by Laura Raine

First there was a **crash**,
followed by a **bash**,
then a **huge enormous thump**
that ended with a **splash.**

Jake was in the garden
in a **heap** below the gate.
Mum was in the kitchen
washing pots and plates.

"What on **earth's** going on out **here?**"
She **asked from behind** the door.

"Oh! **Mum** I must have told **you** this
a thousand times before...

..."I'M SUPER MAGIC LIGHTNING BOY

THE FASTEST KID IN TOWN

AND THIS IS DIXIE THUNDER PAWS

THE MEANEST CAT AROUND!"

"**Ok**" said Mum, playing along,
  she tried to think of something wrong.

"A super **problem** needs your super help,
which can only be solved by your **super self.**
I know you're busy, I beg your pardon,
but there's **something lurking** in the garden.

I need a **hero** to save the day
and make the **baddies** go away."

Jake leapt to it strong and fast.
"A super mission for us at last!"
"Come on" he said and Dixie followed.
Off they went to the **deep, dark hollow.**

Past the **gate** and along the **ledge,**
Is there **something moving** beyond the hedge?

Suddenly a voice cried **"Who goes there?**
Who dares to wander in my lair?"

Jake **peeked** through the **prickly leaves** and saw a moving, **talking tree!**

He leaped in front, so **brave and bold.**
He felt grown up for **eight years old!**

"I'M SUPER MAGIC LIGHTNING BOY
THE FASTEST KID IN TOWN
AND THIS IS DIXIE THUNDER PAWS
THE MEANEST CAT AROUND!"

The tree grew taller, it creaked and cracked.

"Aha so now we meet at last.
I'm **Evil Angus Apple Tree**,
I'm nasty and a brute.
Now just stand still and don't you move
while I pelt you with **this fruit**."

Suddenly the apples came,
one just missed **Jake's shoe.**
Then one nearly hit his head,
some had **worms** in too!

Now **Dixie** didn't like this,
she breathed in and then once more.
She opened up her mouth and
let out the **biggest roar!**

Evil Angus Apple Tree was **frozen** to the spot.
Jake had just the right idea, "I'll show him" he thought.

He grabbed a branch then two then three
and **quickly** ran around the tree.
The tree was stuck, the tree was caught,
the tree **was tied** up in a knot!

"Quick" said Jake, "let's run and hide,
before the tree becomes untied.
Dixie, look at what's ahead,
let's take cover inside Dad's shed."

It was cold. It was dark.
It was quiet. It was eerie.
Jake had to admit
it was **rather scary!**

Jake **bumped** into a pile of stuff
that swirled around a cloud of dust.
Dixie sneezed and gave a cough
then heard a noise from up above!

A creepy voice asked, "who are you?
You're not familiar, are you new?"
Jake was fearless, bold and tough.
He stood up tall and **rhymed it off...**

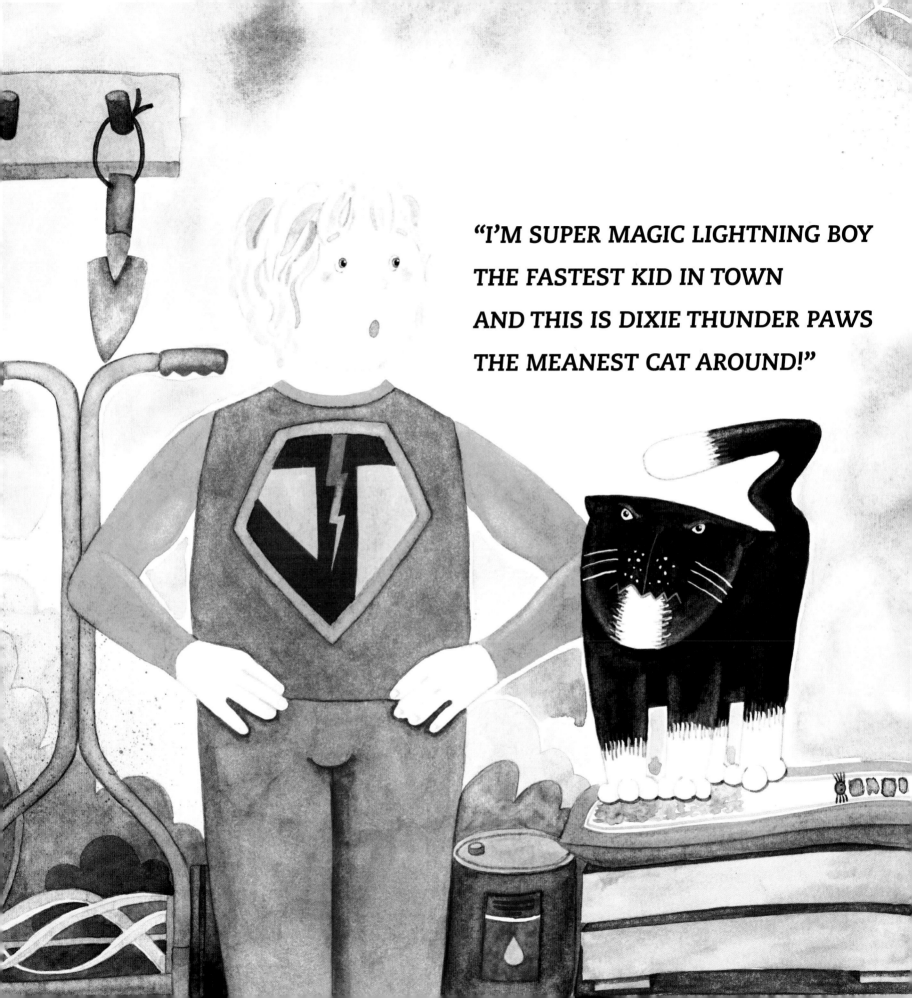

"I'M SUPER MAGIC LIGHTNING BOY
THE FASTEST KID IN TOWN
AND THIS IS DIXIE THUNDER PAWS
THE MEANEST CAT AROUND!"

"**Pleased to meet you,**" the darkness said.
Then all of a **sudden** Jake saw a leg...

Then two, then three, then four, then five,
then six, then seven, then eight, oh my!

Out of the shadows it came unfurled;
the **biggest** spider in the whole, wide world.

It had eight legs and it had eight feet,
a hairy back and pointy teeth.

Well Jake and Dixie **didn't** wait.
They began to plot a **swift escape.**

Jake no longer felt like a hero.
His **bravery** count had dropped to zero.

The **spider** shouted "Don't run away,
I'd like it if you stayed to play!"

But the boy and cat they didn't hear.
They'd already begun to disappear.

They were out the door **quick as a flash**,
along the stones and down the path.

But they ran too fast, their legs got muddled.
They fell head first in a **DIRTY PUDDLE!"**

Jake looked up and saw some shoes.
He knew whose feet were in them too.
"RIGHT YOU TWO THAT'S QUITE ENOUGH
OF THIS SILLY SUPER HERO STUFF.

I'm afraid it's mums who have the last laugh,
now get upstairs...**FOR A LONG HOT BATH!!!**

Even super heroes have to wash!

The End

"Super Magic Lightning Boy'
is an original concept by Scott McIntyre
© Scott McIntyre 2010

Author Scott McIntyre
Illustrated by Laura Raine

Maverick Arts Publishing Ltd
Studio 4, Hardham Mill Park
Pulborough RH20 1LA
+44(0) 1798 875980

©Maverick Arts Publishing Limited (2010)

**PUBLISHED BY MAVERICK ARTS
PUBLISHING LTD**

ISBN 978-1-84886-060-5

arts publishing

www.maverickbooks.co.uk